PROMISES
A Time to Live
by Sue Purkiss

Published by Ransom Publishing Ltd.
Unit 7, Brocklands Farm, West Meon, Hampshire GU32 1JN, UK
www.ransom.co.uk

ISBN   978 178591 258 0
First published in 2016

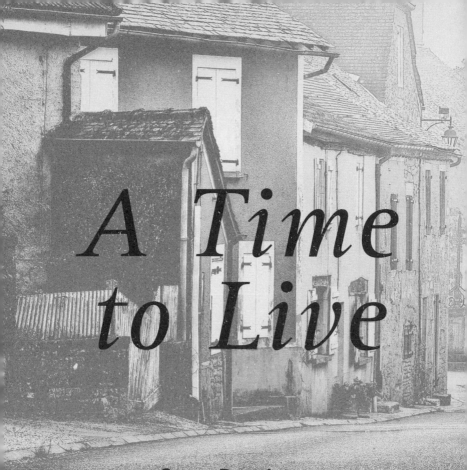

A Time to Live

Sue Purkiss

Ransom

Thursday 30th July, 1942

I'm tired this morning – there was
an air raid last night. The sound of
the engines woke me up and I ran
over to the window and peered out.

In the moonlight I saw planes
flying low – bombers. Were they
British or German? I wasn't sure.

Smaller planes came. They
darted round like angry wasps.
They were fighters. I could tell by

their shape that they were German.

They began to attack the bombers and I saw puffs of smoke and flashes of flame.

Then there was a bigger explosion. It was so bright it made me blink. When I opened my eyes, I saw a tiny white shape drifting down. A parachute. Someone had escaped from the burning plane.

Oh, please let him be all right, I prayed. *Please let him live.*

I wondered if Papa and Maman were watching from their room. Papa wouldn't care if the man lived or died. *Germans, British, they're as bad as each other*, he says.

They all look after their own. None of them cares a bit about France, about us.

But I think he's wrong. Oh, I know the British ran away when the Germans attacked France. But the French ran too. The roads were full of people trying to escape. In the end, they had nowhere to go.

But the Tommies got back to Britain, and they're still fighting. Like we should be.

I keep thinking about the man who jumped. I can't get him out of my mind. The plane that was hit was a big one, a bomber. So he must have been British.

I wonder if he's hurt?

I wonder if he's frightened?

I hope they don't catch him.

At breakfast little brother Pierre was excited. He'd seen the parachute, too.

'Do you think he'll escape?' he said.

'No,' said Papa. 'The Germans will hunt him down. He won't stand a chance.'

'What if someone helps him?' I said. 'Hides him?'

Papa glanced at me. 'They would be very silly if they did,' he said quietly. 'You know the punishment for helping the enemy. Death, at best.'

'But they're not the enemy, are they?' said Pierre, frowning. 'It's the Germans who are the enemy.'

Papa hadn't finished his breakfast, but he got up, pushing his chair back so hard that it fell over.

'For goodness sake! All I want to do is to keep this family safe. And the best way to do that is to keep our heads down and do as we're told. Now – there's work to do. For all of us!'

As he went out, slamming the door, Maman sighed. 'Pierre,' she said. 'Time for school. And Sylvie – *must* you annoy your father so?'

It was *so* unfair. 'I didn't do

anything!' I said. 'I just asked – '

'Yes, I know what you did! Now – can you *just* go and see to the hens?'

So then I stamped out and banged the door too.

As I walked down to the orchard, Pierre cycled past, whistling. He stopped.

'Cheer up,' he said. 'You'll put the hens off their laying with a face like that!'

He can always make me smile. 'I just wish there was something we could *do*!' I said. 'The beastly Germans are all over France, taking our food, telling us what to do – are we just to go along with it?'

He looked at me, his face serious. 'Maybe there is something we can do. The Resistance – '

'Oh, the Resistance!' I scoffed. 'Does it really exist? In Paris maybe, but here in Brittany? I don't think so.'

He shrugged and grinned. 'If you say so!'

I watched him go. He knows something, I can tell. I'll get it out of him later.

The rest of the morning went on as usual. Gather eggs, hang out the washing, bake bread, clean the house, work in the vegetable garden … I almost wish I was still at school too.

Oh, I know we're lucky. If we lived in the town, we'd have to queue for hours to buy food. There's hardly anything in the shops, because the Germans take it all for themselves.

But it's all so dull …

Friday 31st July

Well – not so dull after all! I can't
believe what just happened –
perhaps if I write it down it will
seem more real.

This evening, I went out to shut
the hens up, as I always do. In the
orchard, the leaves whispered in
the breeze and the birds sang.
I leaned against a tree, closing my
eyes, enjoying the peace. And then

suddenly, I had the strangest feeling that someone was watching me.

I opened my eyes and looked around. Nothing. Then, to my right, something rustled in the long grass. I laughed. It was just Minou, the little tabby, my favourite cat.

I scooped her up and nuzzled my face in her soft fur. She wriggled and jumped down.

I turned to go.

And there he was. Tall, thin, his face scratched, no boots on – and a tattered blue-grey uniform. I knew what that meant. He was an English flier.

My mind worked fast. He was

the English flier – the one from last night, the one on the parachute – he must be!

I opened my mouth and he must have thought I was going to scream, because he moved closer and put a finger to his mouth, shaking his head urgently.

'No!' he said. 'Please – s'il vous plaît!'

I didn't need to think about it.

'Don't be afraid,' I said. 'I will help you.'

I spoke in French, of course, but he seemed to understand.

I thought fast. I could take him to the barn where the winter hay is stored. We wouldn't have to go near the house, and no one goes in there at this time of year.

'Come with me,' I said. I felt so excited – at last, there was something I could do!

He followed me, but he kept stumbling. I turned, impatient, but I saw from his face that he was in pain.

'My foot,' he gasped. I nodded. He must have hurt it when he came down. I let him lean on me. He was limping badly, and when we got to the barn he collapsed onto a pile of hay and closed his eyes.

I heard my mother calling me for supper. 'I'll be back soon,' I told him. But his eyes stayed shut. He looked so tired.

He was very young, I saw. Not much older than me. His hair was thick and wavy and blonde. I took a quick look at his ankle. It was swollen and red with a nasty graze.

Maman had made potato omelette for supper. Usually I eat every mouthful, but tonight I just wanted to get through the meal and go back to my airman.

'Can I have that if you don't want it?' asked Pierre.

'What? Oh – yes, if you want.'

I told Maman I would clear the

table and wash the dishes. She looked pleased.

As I put the pots and pans away, I broke off a piece of bread and a hunk of cheese and put them in the pocket of my apron. Then I picked up a bottle of cider and slipped out of the back door. They were listening to the radio in the living room – no one would notice I was gone.

But I was wrong. Someone did notice. When I knelt down beside the airman, I heard an excited voice behind me.

'I knew it! I *knew* something was going on!'

It was Pierre.

Saturday 1st August

The airman's name is Jack Miller.
Pierre is going to help me to look
after him.

I've sworn him to secrecy. He
knows as well as I do that, above
all else, Papa must not find out
about our airman. He would
almost certainly give him up to the
Germans – and I couldn't bear
that.

Our airman is funny and sweet
– so polite. And he makes me
laugh when he speaks French. He
has a terrible accent! He looks sad,
though, when he talks about what
happened.

He was a rear gunner. When
they were hit, the pilot told the
crew that he would keep flying for
as long as he could, so that they
would have a chance to bale out.

'I don't know if the others made
it,' said Jack. 'I didn't see them. But
it was confusing – the noise, and
the lights, and trying to remember
what to do with the parachute.
I thought it was never going to
open, then suddenly it did and it

was so peaceful, just floating down in the moonlight … '

I didn't tell him I only saw one parachute.

Monday 3rd August

It's been two days now, and all's well so far. Pierre is better at stealing food than I am – not that there's much to steal – the Germans take most of what we grow.

Papa doesn't like that, for sure. I think he thought at first that it wouldn't make much difference, having them in charge. But perhaps even he is beginning to wonder.

Pierre came home from school today and told us that there is a new German commandant.

People said the old one wasn't too bad – quite a decent man. He liked music. He stayed in the Mayor's house.

Once, when I walked past, I heard the sound of the piano coming through the open window. It was a sad tune, but I liked it.

And another time I saw him coming out of the house, and he smiled at me and nodded, quite

politely. But he was still German,
so of course I didn't smile back.
Well, I didn't mean to, anyway.

But the new man is said to be
very different. No smiles, no music.

What are we going to do about
Jack? How much longer can we
keep him safe? Sooner or later,
surely Maman will notice that food
is disappearing.

And what if Papa suddenly
decides to go into the barn for
some reason or other?

Sometimes, Jack seems to know
what I'm thinking. He's so sweet,
and his eyes are so blue …

He touched my hand today, and told me not to worry.

'As soon as my foot is better, I'll leave. I promise you. Nothing must happen to you because of me.'

But his foot isn't getting better. It's more swollen, and the redness is going further up his leg. He is pale, and his forehead shines a little with sweat. This is bad, I know. He isn't fit to go anywhere.

And anyway, I don't want him to leave. I like him.

There, I've said it.

But I fear for him ...

Wednesday 5th August

Papa had a letter today, from
Uncle Marc in Paris. As he read it,
a look of shock came over his face.

'How can this be?' he whispered.
'How can such things possibly be?'

He screwed the letter up and
then, without a word to Maman or
me, he strode out of the house as if
he couldn't bear to be inside.

Maman and I looked at each

other, and then she picked up the letter and smoothed it out. As she read it, her eyes went wide and her hand flew to her mouth.

'Maman!' I said. 'What is it? Tell me!'

'Marc says – he says … ' She was silent for a moment and then she began to speak again. 'Do you remember that a Jewish family lived in the flat above them, called the Levins? Things have … become more difficult for the Jews since the Germans came.'

I nodded impatiently. I know this, of course. Hitler hates the Jews. They have to wear a yellow star, and he has stolen their jobs,

their houses, their shops. All of
these things have been happening
in Germany for years now, and
now in France too.

'Marc says … the whole family
was taken away at dawn two
weeks ago. Three children … They
rounded up Jews from all over
Paris. The children were separated
from their parents and kept in a
sports stadium for days – with no
food, no water. Thousands of
them.

'Can you imagine how afraid
they must have been? And now …
they've all been taken away. No
one knows where.'

She looked at me. I have never

seen her look so sad. 'Sylvie – what will happen to those children?' She put her hand out to me and I clutched it.

I made up my mind. 'Maman,' I whispered. 'There is something I have to tell you.'

I told her about Jack, and her eyes opened wide in surprise. Then she stood up.

'Take me to him,' she said firmly. 'There is not a moment to lose. We may not be able to save those children, but we can certainly help this Jack.'

By now, he was only half-conscious,

muttering English words in his sleep.

Maman knelt down and examined his ankle. Then she looked around the barn.

'We must take him inside,' she muttered. 'I can't take proper care of him here.'

'But Papa,' I said. 'What will he say?'

Then I heard my father's voice. It sounded a little rough. Almost as if he had been crying – but that certainly couldn't be.

'I will say, of course we must take care of him. He has been fighting these – these *child-killers*. While I have buried my head in the sand.'

Then, between us, we managed to get Jack into the house and up into the bedroom in the attic.

But it was Papa who took most of the weight.

Friday 7ᵗʰ August

We are very careful. When we
come down from the attic, we take
the steps down and hide them
behind the big wardrobe that
stands in the passageway.

Nothing is left lying about. As
soon as we bring Jack's cup and
plate downstairs, or the basin and
bandages Maman uses to treat his
ankle, we wash them up and put

32

them away. There must be no sign of him, because we never know when the Germans will come.

Since the new commandant arrived, notices keep going up all over town. Orders – we must do this, we mustn't do that. The curfew is earlier now. No one must be outside their houses after 8pm.

And then today Pierre brought home a new poster and flung it on the table. It said that anyone who is caught sheltering the enemy will be shot.

Papa looked at the poster. Then he tore it into tiny pieces and put them into the stove to burn.

'Another time,' he said, 'don't

take the poster down. Someone might see you. Have we any proper coffee left?'

Maman looked surprised. 'A little,' she said. 'I was keeping it for a special occasion.'

He nodded. 'Sylvie, please make some. I will take it up to Jack.'

Pierre and I looked at each other. Up till now, Papa has left it to the rest of us to care for Jack. Maman makes poultices and compresses to put on his ankle, and gives him medicine she makes from herbs. I bathe his forehead and talk to him – silly stuff, about the farm and the people we know. Sometimes, very softly, I sing songs.

But only if he's sleeping. Pierre tells him jokes and asks him what it's like to be a flier. I hear them laughing sometimes. To tell the truth, I feel a little bit jealous then.

Papa carried the coffee upstairs, and we heard him get the ladder out and climb up.

He was up there for an hour.

When he came down, he looked at Maman. 'He is a fine young man,' he said gruffly. 'He will get better?'

Maman nodded. 'The wound was dirty and it was infected. But he's young and strong – he's fighting it. The swelling is starting to go down.'

I went up later. Jack was propped up against his pillows, looking out at the blue sky through the window. 'It is very peaceful here,' he said. 'And you are all so kind to me.' Then he turned and looked at me with those bright blue eyes. 'But I am putting you in danger.'

'Oh no,' I said. 'Out here, no one bothers us much.' I sat on the chair beside his bed. His hand was lying on top of the sheet. I put my own hand on top of his, and said, 'You mustn't worry. You are quite safe, and so are we.'

He smiled, squeezed my hand, and closed his eyes.

Wednesday 12th August

Last night, after supper, Papa
looked round at us all. 'Jack is
getting better,' he said, 'and we
must think about what to do.'

I already had a plan.

'He must become French!'
I said.

They all stared at me, and so
I began to explain. 'We can say he
is a friend of a friend – from Paris,

perhaps. He wants to learn about farming, so he's come to live with us. I can teach him more French – he already knows quite a lot, he learned it at school.'

Maman's eyes lit up. 'Yes! The Germans all speak it so badly anyway – they won't notice if he does too!'

Papa frowned. 'But he has no papers. And people will wonder how he came here – why no one saw him.'

I thought fast. 'We collected him from the station at Rennes. On bicycles. That's far enough away – it would explain why no one saw him arrive.'

'But the papers?'

Pierre cleared his throat.

'I think – I might know someone who can help.'

It turns out that he *did* know more about the Resistance than he's been letting on. He won't tell us anything – he says it's better if we don't know.

Maman was horrified, but Pierre said all he does is take messages sometimes – no one would suspect a fourteen-year-old boy, so it's quite safe.

We all looked at Papa.

I thought he would be angry – furious, in fact. But he wasn't.

He thought for a minute. Then

he nodded, and said, 'Do it, then.'

Maman opened her mouth to speak, but he said, 'These are dangerous times. But we must all do what we can.'

How things have changed, in just a few days!

Monday 25th August

So now Jack Miller is Jacques
Moulin – just the same, only
French instead of English. His foot
is better, and he spends all day out
in the fields with Papa. He wears
old clothes of Papa's – they are too
big, of course, but he manages. His
skin has turned brown in the sun.

Today I took a bottle of wine
out to them, and when he reached

out for it, I noticed that the fine hairs on his arm are golden.

He is not used to the work, but he learns fast. Already, after only a week, he looks fitter and stronger. When he laughs, his teeth are white against his skin.

He helps me with my work too. Today I was getting the sheets off the line, and suddenly he was there, helping me to fold them. He fetches water from the well for Maman, and I can see that she is getting fond of him.

As for Pierre, when he comes home the first thing he does is to look for Jack. Pierre shows him the best places to fish, and Jack tells him stories about England. He comes from a place called Kent, and he says it is a little bit like Brittany. There are orchards and woods and streams, and the sea is never far away.

Monday 7th September

Last night I heard planes again.
Above me, I could hear Jack
pacing up and down. Jack has
taught me a lot about planes, and
I could hear that these were
German bombers, and they were
heading for England.

How must that make him feel?
I wanted to go up to him, but my
parents would hear the noise of the

ladder. I went back to bed, but it was a long time before I got back to sleep.

This morning, he was very quiet.

Papa looked at him. 'You heard the planes last night?'

He nodded. 'If only I knew what was happening!' he burst out. 'I suppose they are flying to London. Over Kent. And my parents … they probably think I'm dead!'

I hadn't thought of that.

This evening, we went for a long

walk together. We talked and talked. He told me about his parents and his sister, and how he would have gone to university if not for the war – he likes books, as I do. The crickets were singing, and an owl swooped low.

We sat down on the bank of a stream and dipped our feet in the water.

It seemed very natural for me to lean against his shoulder, and for him to put his arm round me. As we walked back, we held hands – I felt so happy!

But Papa had a surprise for us when we got back. He was standing next to the radio, looking very pleased with himself. He made sure the curtains were drawn, and then he switched it on. An English voice was speaking. It was the BBC.

We all crouched round the radio – of course, it is not allowed to listen to the BBC.

I couldn't understand all of it, but I knew they were talking about the Battle of Britain, about how the RAF is fighting for its life in the skies above England.

I watched Jack. He looked very serious. When Papa switched it off, Jack said, 'I must go home.'

'But how?' I burst out. 'How can you?'

'I don't know,' he said. 'A boat, perhaps? Surely there must be lots of boats on the coast?'

Papa shook his head. 'Fishing boats are not allowed to work now. I hear that the Germans have destroyed any small boats that are no use to them. That won't work.'

'Then I must walk!'

'Where to?' said Maman, bewildered.

He shrugged. 'Spain, I suppose. We had a lecture about it in training. Spain is not in the war, so they said, if we were shot down, that's where we should make for.'

'But – but it's hundreds of miles away! How could you possibly get there? How would you even know the way?' she said.

'I suppose I'd just head south.' He could see that we all thought it was a ridiculous idea. 'I don't want to,' he burst out. 'Of course I don't!' He looked at me. 'I'd much rather stay here. But it's my duty. I must try to get home – I must!'

'My friends in the Resistance could help,' said Pierre suddenly. 'They've helped other people. I know they have.'

'Oh!' I cried. They all looked at me. But – *home*! I want this to be his home, here on the farm – I don't want him to leave me!

I ran out of the room, tears streaming down my face.

Jack came after me, and suddenly his arms were round me.

'Can't you see?' he said softly. 'I *have* to go. My friends are up there every night, risking their lives. I can't be safe when they're in danger.'

Why not? Why can't he be safe?

Tuesday 8ᵗʰ September

But he isn't safe. I know that now.

Today the Germans came. We heard the roar of the motorcycles coming along the lane. Quick as a flash, Papa told Jack to go and lose himself.

The officer wanted to talk to Papa about quotas. They want more of our meat, more of our produce, more of everything.

When he'd finished, he stood there, his eyes roaming round the farmyard, his stick tapping against his shiny black boot.

'I hear you have a young man working here,' he said, as if it was something of no importance at all.

'Yes,' growled Papa. 'He's from the city. The son of friends. I'm doing him a favour, but to tell the truth, he's not much use. I don't know how much longer I'll keep him on.'

The German nodded. 'We have need of workers in Germany. Our young men are all fighting, and our factories need workers. There, he would be useful.'

My heart thudded. I thought everyone must hear it.

Papa nodded. 'I'll think about that.'

The other man smiled. 'No need to think, my friend. Soon, there will be no choice.'

He nodded to me. I hated how he looked at me with those cold eyes.

I hated *him*.

Wednesday 9th September

And so Pierre has spoken to his friends, and soon, someone will come for Jack, and the Resistance will help him to escape.

I don't know how to bear it.

Thursday 10th September

Pierre looked serious when he came back from school today. 'There's a problem,' he said.

We were all there. Maman was peeling potatoes, I was chopping beans, and Jack and Papa were enjoying a drink of cider after a day's hard work in the sun. We all looked up.

'I don't know what's happened,

but the man who was going to collect Jack can't any longer. We have to get him to Plouval instead – to the house of the priest. And we have to do it now, this evening.'

I gasped and my hand flew to my mouth. So soon!

'I will take him,' said Papa.

Pierre shook his head. 'No. My friend says it will be more natural if I go with him. So it's just a pleasant cycle ride – you know? And he says it's good to have a girl with us.' He frowned. 'I don't really know why, but he seemed very certain.'

This time it was Maman who gasped.

'I'll do it,' I said quickly. 'Of course I will.'

Soon, Jack was ready. He didn't have much to pack.

This might be our last time together. I was determined to treasure every minute.

We rode side by side, glancing at each other from time to time and smiling. Sometimes we even held hands, although that made us wobble a bit, and Pierre told us sternly not to be silly.

We had almost made it, but then just as we reached Plouval, we saw two Germans on the side of

the road, leaning against their
motorbikes. One of them stepped
out in front of us.

'Papieren, bitte.' he said. We all
took out our papers. Just as he took
Jack's, I slipped off my bike and let
out a little cry. They all looked at
me.

'Oh dear!' I said, running my
hand over my ankle. 'I think I've
hurt my foot. Oh, how silly!'

They were only young. They
didn't look much older than Pierre.
When I looked at them from
underneath my eyelashes, they
couldn't do enough to help.

The one who had been going to
look at Jack's papers blushed bright

red, and shoved them back at him
without a second glance.

I allowed him to hold my bike
for me, and when we went on our
way, I waved. I almost blew him a
kiss, but I thought that might be a
bit too much.

'Now I see,' said Pierre
thoughtfully. Jack just grinned.

I can't write about saying goodbye.
It's not goodbye. It can't be. We
had a few minutes to ourselves in
the priest's garden.

I wanted to give him a photo-
graph of me, but he said I mustn't.

'They're not going to catch me,

but if they do, there must be
nothing that could lead them back
to you.'

He put his hand under my chin.
'I'd just be sent to a prisoner of war
camp. But anyone who helped me
– well, you know what would
happen.'

I did. We'd all heard stories of
people who'd been put in prison or
shot for 'helping the enemy'.

'And anyway,' he went on,
'I don't need a picture.' He ran his
fingers over my face and pushed
my hair back. 'How could I possibly
forget what you look like? And
I *will* come back for you. You'll see.'

'You'd better,' I said fiercely.

'Promise you won't get yourself killed. Because this isn't a time to die. It's a time to live! You *must* stay alive – for me … '

Soon, Pierre and I were cycling home.

'We'd better go the back way,' I said. 'Just in case those clowns are still there.'

'You're pretty good at this,' said Pierre, smiling.

'Yes,' I said. 'I am, aren't I? I think you'd better say that to your friends. I think I'm going to be quite useful, don't you?'

Friday 25th May, 1945

And I *have* been useful. I've
forgotten how many escapers I've
helped on the long journey to
Spain.

Each of us has done our bit.

And I've done other things too,
particularly in the last year or two,
as liberation came closer. We've all
done what we can, and I'm proud
of us.

But now, at last, it's all over.
And last week, a letter came –
from England. From Kent. He did
it! He stayed alive!

Soon, the gate will swing open,
and there he'll be, my airman.

Keeping his promise, as I always
knew he would.

MORE GREAT READS IN THE PROMISES SERIES

Yasmin's Journey
by Miriam Halahmy

Fifteen-year-old Yasmin lives with her parents and younger brother Ali in a small town in Syria.

The country is at war and Yasmin is forced to leave Syria with Ali to find a new life for them both.

Travelling through the refugee camps of Turkey and Greece, Yasmin strikes up a friendship with sixteen-year-old Kamal. Can they all find peace and safety together?

My Sister's Perfect Husband
by Rosemary Hayes

Laila's older sister Mina is eighteen, and her Pashtun family feel it's time they found her a husband.

They introduce her to several suitable young men, but Mina scowls at each one, putting them off as much as she can.

So Laila sets about finding the perfect husband for her sister.